LOS ANGELES

MICHAEL E. GOODMAN

THE HISTORY OF THE

DODGERS

CREATIVE EDUCATION

Published by Creative Education
123 South Broad Street, Mankato, Minnesota 56001
Creative Education is an imprint of The Creative Company

Designed by Rita Marshall
Editorial assistance by John Nichols

Photos by: Allsport Photography, AP/Wide World, Corbis-Bettmann, Focus
on Sports, Fotosport, SportsChrome.

Library of Congress Cataloging-in-Publication Data

Goodman, Michael.
The History of the Los Angeles Dodgers / by Michael Goodman.
p. cm. — (Baseball)
Summary: Highlights players, managers, and memorable games in the history
of the baseball team that began in Brooklyn in 1890 and moved to the West
Coast in 1958.
ISBN: 0-88682-912-7

1. Los Angeles Dodgers (Baseball team)—History—Juvenile literature.
[1. Los Angeles Dodgers (Baseball team)—History. 2. Baseball—History.]
I. Title. II. Series: Baseball (Mankato, Minn.)

GV875.L6G67   1999
796.357'64'0979494—dc21   97-1875

First edition

9 8 7 6 5 4 3 2 1

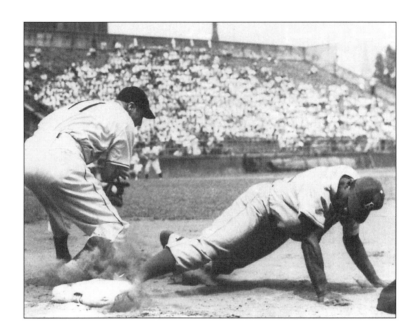

Hall of Fame manager Tommy Lasorda may have said it best when he stated, "The book of baseball would be only four pages long without the Dodgers." Lasorda's statement is an exaggeration to be sure, but indeed, the Dodgers' franchise has been one of the finest in baseball, if not in all sports, for more than 100 years. Twenty-one National League pennants and six World Series titles are evidence of the club's excellence over the decades, as are the 47 former Dodgers who are now members of the National Baseball Hall of Fame.

The Dodgers' history began in 1890 in Brooklyn, New

The legendary Jackie Robinson.

York. The citizens of the blue-collar borough of New York City fell in love with the ballclub, and the franchise enjoyed great success there until 1958. That year, in a move that broke millions of Brooklyn hearts, the Dodgers left New York for sunny Los Angeles, California. Since then, the team has continued its winning ways and has further built upon the rich tradition begun by its Brooklyn predecessors. From the stars of the past, like Jackie Robinson and Sandy Koufax, to the stars of the present, like Charles Johnson and Hideo Nomo, the "Dodgers' way" has meant only one thing—winning. And Dodgers fans everywhere have come to expect nothing less.

1 9 0 1

"Wee" Willie Keeler topped the 200-hit mark for the second straight season with 202.

FROM "BRIDEGROOMS" TO "BUMS"

The Dodgers have been big winners on the West Coast, but their luck wasn't always good during their early years. The team wasn't called the Dodgers at first, but was known as the "Bridegrooms" because so many of the players had been married during the previous year. The newlyweds got off to a good start in baseball, winning the championship in 1890, their first year in the National League. But the honeymoon was soon over. Nine years passed before Brooklyn won the league title again.

When the American League was formed in 1900, several of Brooklyn's best players jumped to the new league. The Dodgers, who were also known as the "Superbas" until 1905, once again fell on hard times. For the first 15 years of the new century, the Brooklyn club finished in every spot except first place. In one terrible year, they finished dead

Former Dodger Hideo Nomo.

Jake Daubert won the NL batting title and became the first Dodger to be named league MVP.

last, 56½ games behind the league-leading New York Giants. There was even talk of moving the team to Baltimore during this period. However, team president Charley Ebbets managed to borrow enough money to purchase the club. Then he borrowed more money to begin building a new stadium that would hold more fans and help him repay his loans.

The new stadium opened in 1913. Ebbets was asked what he planned to name the building. "Washington Park, same as the old place, I guess," he said. Then someone suggested, "Why not Ebbets Field?" Never known as a modest man, Ebbets eagerly agreed.

The following year, Ebbets took another important step forward. He found the right manager for his club—a chubby, former big-league catcher named Wilbert Robinson, who led the team for the next 18 years.

Robinson was well-liked by his players and the fans, who called him "Uncle Willie." The Dodgers even acquired an additional nickname in the manager's honor—the "Robins." The Dodgers/Robins won two pennants early in Robinson's Brooklyn career, in 1916 and 1920, then settled back into the bottom half of the National League standings for the next 20 years. It was 1941 when the team finished atop the National League again. By then, Robinson was long gone, and the team was known exclusively as the Dodgers—a name taken from the skill Brooklyn fans displayed at "dodging" in and out of the city's congested streets and subways on their way to ball games.

During the fruitless 1920s and '30s, the Dodgers played uneven baseball, finishing no better than fifth 14 times. The caliber of play may not have been top quality, but the colorful cast of characters who wore the Brooklyn uniform kept events at Ebbets Field entertaining. The team didn't win any pennants, but it did win the hearts of its fans, who lovingly called their Dodgers "dem bums." Laughing until they cried, Dodgers fans ended each season with the hopeful thought, "Wait 'till next year."

One of the most beloved players—and one of the daffiest—was Babe Herman. Herman was a great hitter who, during two back-to-back seasons, batted .381 and .393 respectively. But in the field and on the bases, Herman had his problems. His feet always seemed to get tangled as he went back to catch fly balls, and at least once the ball landed on his head instead of in his glove.

Herman's most famous goof occurred during a game in 1926. The bases were loaded with no outs when Herman came to bat. He lashed a hard shot toward the right-field wall. The runners thought it might be caught, so they stayed close to their bases. The ball hit the wall, however, and then the confusion began. The runner from third scored easily, but the runner from second got partway to home plate and decided to return to third base to play it safe. The runner from first also arrived at third base. As if the base weren't crowded enough, along came Herman. Running as fast as he could with his head down, Herman raced around second and slid into third with what he thought was a triple. Instead, the third baseman tagged out Herman and the runner who had started on first. Imagine that: Herman had become the first player ever to triple into a double play. No wonder Brooklyn fans called them "dem bums."

For the seventh consecutive season, Dodger ace Dazzy Vance led the NL in strikeouts.

Lead-off man Brett Butler's speed . . .

. . . was as dangerous as Dusty Baker's power.

A few days later, a fan who arrived late for a game at Ebbets Field asked a nearby fan how the Dodgers were doing. The neighbor said, "They've got three men on base." The first fan replied, "Really? Which base?" Dodgers fans had to have a sense of humor back then.

1 9 4 5

Brooklyn star Eddie Stanky drew an NL-record 148 walks during the season.

ROBINSON CHANGES BASEBALL HISTORY

No one laughed at the Dodgers once the 1940s began. Fiery new manager Leo Durocher helped develop a team that combined power with solid pitching to take Brooklyn back to the top of the National League. The team won the pennant in 1941, placed a close second in 1942, and finished in a tie for first place at the end of the 1946 season, only to lose to the St. Louis Cardinals in a playoff series. But the best was yet to come. The Dodgers were about to change baseball history forever.

During the mid-1940s, Branch Rickey took over as general manager of the Dodgers. Rickey was famous for his ability to build winning teams. He had some other important qualities, too: he wasn't afraid to be daring, and he believed that black athletes deserved an equal opportunity to play with whites. Rickey was determined to eliminate the barrier that kept black players from reaching the major leagues and restricted them to playing in Negro leagues.

During the 1945 season, Rickey sent a scout to Kansas City to report on a shortstop named Jackie Robinson playing for a Negro league team there. Rickey knew that Robinson was a top athlete—he had starred in baseball, football, and track at UCLA—and a very intelligent person. He wondered, however, if Robinson was a strong enough man to handle the harsh treatment he would face as the first black player in major league baseball.

Before he signed Jackie Robinson to a contract with the Dodgers, Rickey had a long talk with the young player. He said, "I need more than a great player. I need a man who has a special kind of courage. If a guy slides hard into you at second base or curses at you, I wouldn't blame you if you came up swinging, but you would set the cause back 20 years. I want a man with courage enough not to fight back. Can you do that?"

Robinson was a proud man who cared about improving conditions for black people and black athletes. He agreed to hold his temper in check and joined the Dodgers in 1947. In that first year, he took a lot of abuse from other players around the league. Robinson didn't fight back; he just played harder. He led the league in stolen bases and was second in runs scored. He was also named Rookie of the Year. In 1947, and for the next 10 years, his speed, talent, and special fire helped the Dodgers become tops in the National League year after year.

More importantly though, Robinson gave hope to black children everywhere. "Before Jackie played, none of us kids would even have dreamed of playing in the big leagues," explained future Hall-of-Famer Frank Robinson. "But when he made it, it gave us all hope that the world was coming around a little."

Jackie Robinson didn't turn Brooklyn into a winner all by himself. Rickey also brought in rookie outfielders Carl Furillo and Duke Snider, first baseman Gil Hodges, and two other

1 9 4 9

Shortstop "Pee Wee" Reese was named the Dodgers' first captain ever by general manager Branch Rickey.

1 9 5 6

Duke Snider set a Dodgers single-season record by blasting 43 home runs.

fine black players—catcher Roy Campanella and pitcher Don Newcombe—to go along with such veterans as shortstop "Pee Wee" Reese and pitcher "Preacher" Roe. The Dodgers became kings of the National League and super-heroes to nearly every baseball fan in Brooklyn. They were not called bums anymore.

The one thing the Dodgers couldn't do, however, was beat their New York rivals from the American League, the Yankees. The Dodgers and Yankees faced off in the 1947, 1949, 1952, and 1953 World Series. Each time, the Yankees came out on top.

Brooklyn finally turned the tables in 1955. The World Series that year was one of the most exciting ever, ending in a seventh-game showdown. A great catch by left fielder Sandy Amoros saved at least two Yankee runs from scoring, and pitcher Johnny Podres held the Yankees in check for an exciting 2–0 win. For the first time in Brooklyn baseball history, the beloved Dodgers were world champs.

Little did the fans know, however, that this would be Brooklyn's last championship. After the 1957 season, Dodgers owner Walter O'Malley decided to move the team to Los Angeles. There he could build a stadium larger than Ebbets Field and permit even more Dodgers fans to see their heroes play. An era had ended, but a new one had begun.

KOUFAX STARTS A NEW WINNING TRADITION

The great Dodger teams of the 1950s featured some of the best pitchers in the National League. One pitcher who never made it big in Brooklyn, however, was a young

Former Dodgers great Orel Hershiser.

Maury Wills, a star of the '60s.

fireballer named Sandy Koufax, who had grown up there. In his first three seasons with the Dodgers in New York, Koufax won only nine games and lost 10. He didn't do that much better in his first three seasons in Los Angeles either, winning 27 and losing 30.

Koufax could always throw hard, but he struggled for control during his first few campaigns. The Dodgers almost gave up on him. Finally, pitching coach Joe Becker took him aside. "Trying superspeed every time you're in a jam hurts you," Becker said. "You have to learn how to relax. You should also throw your curve sometimes. You can get it over."

The next time he was on the mound, Koufax found himself in a tough situation. The bases were loaded with no one out. He decided to relax and use his curveball for a change. "I'll never forget that," Koufax said later. "I got out of the inning without a run scoring."

Once he learned to blend speed with control, Koufax began to look like the great Hall-of-Famer he'd soon become. Between 1960 and 1966, Koufax was unstoppable and almost unhittable. He led the league in wins three times, in strikeouts four times, and in earned-run average five times. He threw four no-hitters, including one perfect game.

In 1963, Koufax won 25 games and lost only five. He struck out more than 300 batters and pitched 11 shutouts, too. He was an easy choice as the National League Most Valuable Player and earned the Cy Young Award as the best pitcher in baseball. He also led the Dodgers to a remarkable four-game sweep of the dreaded Yankees in the World Series.

Sandy Koufax had three more great seasons with the

1 9 6 5

The amazing Sandy Koufax continued to baffle hitters, setting a Dodgers record with 382 strikeouts.

Steve Sax, a strong defensive player (pages 18-19).

Dodgers, leading them back to the World Series in 1965 and 1966. During this period, the team also featured Hall of Fame pitcher Don Drysdale, the fine hitting of first baseman Ron Fairly and outfielders Tommy Davis and Willie Davis, and the blazing speed of Maury Wills, the first man ever to steal more than 100 bases in a season.

1 9 7 7

In his first full season as the Dodgers' skipper, Tommy Lasorda led the team to the World Series.

After the 1966 season, elbow problems caused Koufax to retire from baseball at the age of 31. His arm hurt terribly after every game, and he had to soak his elbow in a bucket of ice just to be able to move it normally. Doctors told him that if he continued to pitch, he risked never being able to lift his arm again. In 1966, his last season, Koufax had one final remarkable year. He won 27 games, struck out 313 batters, and had the lowest earned-run average in the National League in more than 25 years (1.73). Then he called it quits. Five years later, he was elected to the Hall of Fame at age 36, the youngest player ever given that honor.

"FERNANDOMANIA" SPARKS DODGERS

With Sandy Koufax's retirement, the Dodgers embarked on an eight-year dry spell with no World Series appearances. The team lost lots of games, but the Dodgers' management wasn't worried. The club was busily developing future stars in its minor-league system. Dodgers fans in sunny California remained patient as they waited for the bright future to arrive.

By the mid-1970s, Los Angeles had the best young infield in baseball. Steve Garvey, an excellent hitter and a top fielder at first base, was named league MVP in 1974. Davey Lopes was a solid second baseman and lead-off hitter with blazing speed. Bill Russell became a consistent shortstop, while Ron Cey (called the "Penguin" because of his short, stumpy, bowed legs) fielded well at third base and became one of the top RBI men in the league. These four players helped the Dodgers win National League pennants in 1977 and 1978. Each time, however, the Dodgers lost to the Yankees in the World Series. Then came 1981 and the arrival of a 20-year-old pitcher from Mexico named Fernando Valenzuela, the finest left-hander to pitch in Los Angeles since Koufax.

Valenzuela didn't look or pitch like Koufax. Koufax was tall and slim; Valenzuela was short and round. Koufax spoke with a Brooklyn accent; Valenzuela spoke Spanish and little English. Koufax threw fastballs and hard curves; Valenzuela

1 9 7 8

Steve Garvey banged out 202 hits to lead the National League for the season.

The incredible Fernando Valenzuela.

Kirk Gibson provided power and speed in the '80s.

threw a screwball that drove right-handed batters crazy. The two great pitchers had one thing in common, however; they both knew how to win.

In fact, Valenzuela couldn't lose for the first two months of the 1981 season. He started out the year with an 8–0 record and ended up leading the league in shutouts and strikeouts. He also became the first player ever to win the Rookie of the Year and Cy Young awards in the same season.

The whole nation caught "Fernandomania" that year, with record crowds turning out in every stadium in which Valenzuela pitched. Valenzuela became a special hero to the many Hispanics living in Southern California. Manager Tommy Lasorda said, "As much as we loved him, his impact was greatest on the Mexican community. He was the greatest hero they ever had."

Valenzuela and the Dodgers kept winning in 1981, and the team made a return trip to the World Series against the Yankees. Valenzuela saved his most heroic performance of the year for the third game of the series. The Yankees had won the first two games and were looking to make fast work of the Dodgers. Tired from the long year and the exhausting playoffs, Valenzuela didn't have his best stuff that night. The Yankees rocked him for four quick runs in the first three innings. But he held on. Lasorda was tempted to take out his struggling star, but he didn't.

"Leaving him in the game was one of the most difficult managerial decisions I've ever had to make," Lasorda said. "Traditional strategy called for me to take him out, but I just couldn't. I knew he was throwing the ball well, and . . . it was the year of Fernandomania. He pitched and got into and

1 9 8 4

Pitcher Alejandro Pena led the National League in ERA with a mark of 2.48.

23

out of more jams than a snake charmer without his flute, but I just couldn't go out there and get him."

Valenzuela rewarded his manager's faith by shutting down the Yankees for the rest of the game, as his teammates came back for a 5–4 win. That victory inspired the Dodgers to take the next three games from the Yankees as well and capture the World Series. Now Koufax and Valenzuela had something else in common: they had each led the Dodgers to World Series triumphs over the Yankees.

1 9 8 8

In a record-breaking season, Orel Hershiser was the Dodgers' lone All-Star Game representative.

"BULLDOG" HERSHISER GIVES DODGERS NEW BITE

After Valenzuela and the Dodgers had their dream season in 1981, Los Angeles came back to reality for the

Pedro Guerrero, a serious threat to the opposition.

next few years. Once again, the Dodgers' management didn't worry or rest on its past success. It began rebuilding the team from the bottom, developing talent in the minor leagues. The Dodgers continued to bring in top rookies throughout the 1980s, including second baseman Steve Sax and pitchers Ramon Martinez and Orel Hershiser.

When Hershiser first made it to the big leagues, the skinny youngster didn't look very intimidating on the mound, so Lasorda decided to help. He gave Hershiser the nickname "Bulldog" to remind him to be a tough pitcher. Hershiser took the nickname to heart and in his second year won 19 games and lost only three to help the Dodgers win the '85 Western Division title. Three years later, he had his own dream season.

Hershiser was remarkable in 1988. During one stretch at the end of the year, he pitched six consecutive shutouts (hurling 59 straight scoreless innings in all) and broke the record for consecutive scoreless innings set in 1968 by Dodgers great Don Drysdale.

Hershiser continued his mastery in the playoffs against the New York Mets and in the World Series against the Oakland A's, and he was elected the Most Valuable Player in each series. After the season, one sportswriter noted, "Hershiser may never have another year like 1988—maybe nobody ever will!"

As great as Hershiser was against the A's, the moment that stands out most from the 1988 World Series was a dramatic pinch-hit home run by Kirk Gibson with two outs in the bottom of the ninth inning of game one.

Gibson had joined the Dodgers as a free agent before the

1 9 9 0

In his first full major-league season, Ramon Martinez posted a 20–6 record and a 2.92 ERA.

One of the game's best catchers, Charles Johnson (pages 26-27).   25

1 9 9 6

LA catcher Mike Piazza had a monster year, batting .336 and blasting 36 home runs.

1988 season. His fiery spirit earned him the National League MVP award that year, but his reckless playing style resulted in a painful leg injury near the end of the season. He made only one batting appearance during the World Series, but he certainly made it count.

Gibson was limping severely as he made his way to the plate. The Dodgers had a man on but were trailing 4–3 and were one out away from losing the game. Unable to put any weight on his sore leg, Gibson swung weakly at two pitches. Down to his last strike, the hobbled star bore down and boomed the next delivery from Oakland's star reliever Dennis Eckersley into the right-field stands for the game-winner. The A's never recovered from that blow, and Los Angeles, behind Hershiser and the other Dodgers hurlers, took three of the next four games to earn another world championship.

JOHNSON, BONILLA FUEL DODGERS HOPES

The Dodgers remained a contender in the National League through the mid-1990s, but with the passage of time came a changing of the guard in Los Angeles. Fernando Valenzuela, Orel Hershiser, and Kirk Gibson moved on to other teams through free agency, and in 1996 Tommy Lasorda retired from the Dodgers, ending a 20-year managerial career that included two world championships, four National League pennants, and eight National League Western Division titles. Losses of players like these would cripple most organizations, but not the Dodgers. "No one person, and I mean no one, is bigger than Dodgers baseball," proclaimed

Lasorda at his Hall of Fame induction in 1997. "The names change, but the Dodgers' tradition remains forever." The newest generation of Dodgers heroes, led by catcher Charles Johnson and starting pitcher Hideo Nomo, looks ready to add another chapter to the franchise's fabled history.

For five-plus seasons the Dodgers were led by Mike Piazza, the 1993 Rookie of the Year and five-time All-Star catcher whose powerful bat astounded both fans and competitors alike. The baseball world was naturally stunned when, early in the 1998 season, Los Angeles traded the game's best-hitting catcher to the Florida Marlins (who traded him to the New York Mets a week later). It was a bargain, however, as the Dodgers received perhaps baseball's finest defensive catcher, Charles Johnson.

1 9 9 7

Hideo Nomo became the fastest pitcher in major-league history to record 500 strikeouts (in only 444.2 innings).

Although Johnson was not expected to hit with the power or consistency of Piazza, the Dodgers hope their new 220-pound, 6-foot-2 catcher will continue to mow down base-stealers with his cannon arm. Johnson's unmatched skill behind the plate earned him three Gold Glove awards with the Marlins. "If stealing bases is a crime, Charles Johnson is RoboCop. He's the law out there," joked Montreal Expos speedster Delino DeShields.

The Dodgers' tradition of offering opportunity to people of all races, creeds, and colors continued in 1995 when Hideo Nomo became only the second-ever Japanese born player to make a major-league team. Nomo wowed the baseball world and delighted Los Angeles' large Asian community with his quirky corkscrew delivery and devastating split-fingered fastball. "The guy's not a gimmick," explained Colorado Rockies slugger Larry Walker. "When he gets the

Slugging outfielder Gary Sheffield.

Dodgers ace Ramon Martinez.

Newly acquired third baseman Bobby Bonilla was expected to add a big bat to the Dodgers' lineup.

fastball and the splitter working together, he's untouchable." Nomo was untouchable his rookie season in 1995, going 13–6 with 236 strikeouts and an ERA of 2.54.

With his remarkable rookie season, Nomo became the fourth in a series of five consecutive Dodgers to be named National League Rookie of the Year. (First baseman Eric Karros in '92, Piazza in '93, outfielder Raul Mondesi in '94, and outfielder Todd Hollandsworth in '96 were the others.) "That's what makes this organization so special," explained Nomo through an interpreter. "We have players from all around the world, and although we may speak different languages, we all understand baseball very well."

With the farm system producing All-Star talent seemingly every year, the Dodgers' future looks as promising as the organization's past. "We've got a lot to live up to," explained new Dodgers manager Bill Russell. "Success in this organization is measured by championships, and before this group is done, I feel we will reach that level."

For Dodgers fans, the "wait 'till next year" might not be a very long wait at all.